Donovan's Tales

The Magic Mirror

Written
by
Jake Somerset

Illustrated
by
Trinity Burns

Stonegate Tales
Oklahoma City, Oklahoma, USA

For Stonegate Stars that always shine, but especially for those whose lights are now among the heavens shining bright through memories they left behind for the rest of us.

"You'll be a great help setting up camp," the Princess assured him, "We'll need a place that is out of sight where we can rest."

"But…"Ashe began.

"A good soldier follows orders," Rhys interrupted.

"Yes," Bevin added, "You want to be a good Chimeran trooper."

"Yes, sir," the youth reluctantly said.

Kaylyn stated, "Let's be on our way."

Chapter 12

The town of Bryn Mawr was bustling with people.

"It appears we are not quite alone in our search," Dayan commented, "There are more people here than even I expected."

Kaylyn sighed as she glanced at the crowded streets, "I was hoping there would be only a few but at least we have an advantage."

"Advantage?" Dayan asked.

"We need to find a talking bird," she answered, "Specifically, a hawk."

"Ah, alright," the wizard added, "A hawk, but where do we begin to look for him?"

The Princess looked up and saw the tavern just ahead. "Possibly we can get some information there. If there is a hawk that is a talking bird around this village, someone there would know."

A man opened the grog shop door and staggered down the street. Nearby two others were arguing loudly and began shoving each other. Another sat by the door side begging.

"The place doesn't look too inviting," Bevin commented.

Kaylyn nodded, "We need to be on guard."

The group entered and looked about. The place was teeming with people. The noise was nearly deafening.

"What do you want!" demanded a man from behind the bar.

"What?" the Princess shouted.

"I said, what do you want!" he bellowed.

"A place to sit down and possibly something to drink," Kaylyn yelled.

The barkeep motioned. "There's a table in the back over there," he growled, "I'll bring some grog to you soon enough."

The companions made their way through the crowd and found the table.

"Getting information in here may prove to be difficult," Dayan stated.

"And who can we trust?" Rhys added.

Kaylyn looked around. She took a deep breath. "This may prove to be harder than I anticipated," she thought.

A young man approached the table. He stopped and looked them over. "My, my," he smiled, "more mirror hunters."

Kaylyn shifted in her chair and slowly drew a deep breath. "What are you talking about?" she asked, "We're just simple travelers passing through." She hoped her answer would satisfy the man.

"Do you really think you are fooling anyone?" he taunted, "Simple travelers don't come armed like you are. Bow, arrows, swords, you are definitely mirror hunters."

Kaylyn realized their weapons may have given them away. "Would you be so kind as to move on," she hissed.

"Why should I?" he asked.

"We don't need our presence announced to the world," she growled.

The man laughed, "This tavern is full of mirror hunters. Besides, your group looks a bit pathetic. If you think these two boys, a shabby old man, a dog, and a bird will help you find the treasure, then you are a fool."

Shamar growled at him.

"Quiet, Shamar," Kaylyn said, "We already have too much attention, especially since this person has informed the entire tavern."

The wolf bowed his head and quieted.

"You speak to that animal as if he understands you," the man said.

"You would be surprised," the Princess stated.

"Where are you from?" he questioned her.

"Why do you want to know?" she asked.

"It's just the manner in which you are dressed," he answered, "You're definitely not from around here."

"Chimera," Kaylyn reluctantly replied.

"Ah, the enchanted land," the young man commented, "I now know why you seek it." He leaned close to the Princess. "Would you like to know where it is hidden?" he whispered.

Bevin and Rhys let their hands fall to the hilt of their swords. Just then the barkeep delivered the glasses of grog. Everyone quieted and sat back in their chairs.

"I seriously doubt you would have any information of use to us," she answered as the barkeep walked away.

"You might be surprised," the man insisted. Kaylyn eyed her antagonist. He looked harmless enough. She could see no weapons. Finally she said, "I told you, we're not here looking for any mirror. We are looking for a talking bird."

"A talking bird in Arcadia. Now that is interesting. What kind of bird?" he insisted.

"A hawk," she answered, "His name is Nathan.".

"You have found him," he smiled, "I am Nathan Hawk."

Kaylyn looked at Dayan. He slightly shook his head and returned a look of doubt. The Princess eyed the man suspiciously.

"Not that I question your truthfulness, but do you have any proof?" she asked.

"Well, I wouldn't drink any of the grog they just brought to you," Hawk replied.

"Why not?" the Princess demanded.

"It's drugged," he answered.

Kaylyn looked at Dayan. The magician pulled the glass close and slid the tip of his wand out of his right sleeve. He touched the glass with the wand and a powder rose to the surface of the brew. He slid the glass over to his granddaughter.

"Looks like it is a sleeping powder," he whispered.

She frowned.

Hawk watched and then said, "Is that enough proof?"

Kaylyn nodded. She leaned toward him. "If you are Nathan Hawk, you have some information that very few people know of and we need," she quietly said.

"You and many others," Hawk answered in a low tone, "but I will help you."

"Why offer the information to us?" Dayan asked, looking about to see if anyone was listening.

"First, you're Chimerans. They are known to be trustworthy," Hawk answered, barely able to be heard in the noise of the tavern, "Then look around us. Everyone you see is looking for the mirror. They all want it for the wrong reasons." He lowered his voice, "That gaudy dressed fellow behind me is Jaques the Vile also known as the scourge of the Franks. Those with him are his band of marauders. They want the mirror to help them find cities to raid for whatever wealth may be found there. They are nothing more than cut throats and murderers." Kaylyn let her eyes wander over the men. There was not a friendly face among them. Each appeared to be battle scarred in one way or another. She could see that they each carried a sword.

Nathan turned a bit. "Those short bearded fellows to my left are dwarves. I assume they seek it so they can make themselves rich."

The Princess looked at them. They appeared to be like short, muscular men. At least they didn't look quite so threatening but she saw they carried swords also,

Nathan leaned back. "Now that black haired brute to my right is Count Gregor of the Huns. He wants to use it to his advantage to conquer other lands. He is known as one of the most ruthless killers one could ever meet."

Kaylyn saw a man who was obviously a warrior yet he did not appear to be carrying a weapon. She trembled a bit when she saw that he was staring at them. His face showed no expression. She felt as if she was looking into the eyes of a cold blooded killer.

Hawk then took a deep breath. "Worst of all is in that dark back corner," he shivered, "Goblins. I believe they are allied with Count Gregor but one can never know with goblins. Who knows what their reason is in finding the mirror."

The Princess looked to the corner and a cold chill went down her back for there she could see four green hulking monsters. Seeing the beasts brought back memories of doing battle with them. She took a deep breath and turned her attention back to Nathan.

"What of the others here?" Kaylyn asked as she looked about.

"All seekers of the magic mirror," he answered, "but, in my opinion, none as dangerous as those I have mentioned."

"You could have easily sold your information to the highest bidder," Dayan commented.

"True, but once they had the information, they would have killed me and taken back their money," Hawk answered.

"We could do the same," Dayan stated.

"But you won't," Nathan smiled, "Again, you're Chimerans."

"What do you want out of this?" Kaylyn demanded.

"To use the mirror occasionally," he answered, "for my own purposes."

His answer was vague and unsettling but Kaylyn pressed on. "You're sure no one else here knows you have this information?" she quietly asked.

"No one," Hawk answered in a whisper, "Do we have a deal?"

Kaylyn looked at her grandfather. He nodded. She turned back to Nathan, "We have a deal."

"We should probably leave," Dayan suggested.

The Princess nodded. The group stood and began to make their way out.

"Hey!" the barkeep yelled, "Pay for the grog!"

"But we haven't as much as touched it," Kaylyn protested, "Allow someone else the privilege of drinking it."

"You owe me for the grog!" the barkeep roared once again.

"Let me handle this," Dayan said to his granddaughter. The wizard walked back to the table and picked up one glass. He stepped up to the barkeep. "I will offer to pay for everyone's refreshments today if you will but drink this one," he smiled as he slid the glass across the counter. The bartender hesitated. He stared at Dayan and then frowned. He motioned for two thugs to come to his aid. They approached with clubs in hand. Kaylyn spoke up, "Sir, we don't want to get any blood on your floor. Might my two young men discuss this matter with your fellows outside?"

The barkeep laughed and said, "Certainly."

The two brutes exited the tavern with Rhys and Bevin following. In a few moments there were noises of a fight. Howls of pain followed. The barkeep smiled until Bevin and Rhys walked back through the door. The brutes did not follow. Dayan grinned. "Time for you to take your drink now," he said.

"And if I don't?" the bartender growled.

Rhys laid a blood stained club on the bar. His message was clear.

The bar keep shakily picked up the grog and sipped at it. He put his hand to his head and began to teeter. He reached out and grabbed the bar but it did no good. He fell to the floor.

The tavern got very quiet. Everyone put their drinks down.

"Drink heartily!" Dayan called out as he laid some coins on the bar.

Kaylyn smiled and the group left.

Outside the tavern Nathan commented, "Those two young men handled themselves well."

"They should," Kaylyn replied, "They are Chimeran soldiers. They have faced the likes of Vikings and Goblins." They walked to the edge of town. "By the way," the Princess asked, "Why did that barkeep drug our drinks?"

"Probably to eliminate some of the competition for the mirror," Hawk answered, "I would not be surprised if he was in the pay of Count Gregor."

"Do you think ours were the only ones that were drugged?" she questioned.

"I would be willing to wager that most of those patrons of the tavern will have an extremely long nap," Nathan answered. "Where can we go that is safe to talk?" he asked.

"I have a house just outside of town," Dayan suggested.

Kaylyn nodded and led the way.

Little did they know that there were eyes on their every move.

Chapter 13

As they reached the edge of town, Kaylyn spoke to her Falcon, "Fatima, scout ahead please."

The bird bowed her head and said, "As you wish." She opened her wings and flew off. Shamar asked, "Should I take the lead back to camp?"

Kaylyn nodded and the wolf trotted out in front of the company.

Nathan gulped, "Did those animals just talk?"

"Of course," the Princess answered, "They're Chimerans." She smiled for she saw the bewildered look on Nathan's face. "Now, tell me, where is the mirror?" she asked.

Hawk nervously glanced around him. "I would feel safer at the house," he said.

They walked in silence for some time. Finally the hut came into view.

Kaylyn called out, "Donovan! Ashe! We're back."

"You left some of your company here?" Hawk asked. Then his mouth fell open and his eyes widened when he saw a dragon followed by a youth with a bow step out of the woods.

The Princess laughed, "You have no need to fear the boy. He won't hurt you. Now my dragon friend is another matter, especially if you have lied to me."

Nathan took a deep breath. "I swear to you that the information I have is true," he stammered, still eyeing the dragon.

"Who is this?" Donovan asked as he walked up to the Princess.

"This," she answered, "is the hawk we sought."

The dragon frowned.

"He is named Nathan Hawk," the Princess explained, "Apparently Queen Snow White's sheriff just assumed it was a bird."

The dragon leaned down and looked Nathan in the face. "You know the location of the mirror?" he asked.

Hawk could feel the dragon's hot breath and anxiously nodded.

"We're safe here," Dayan said, "Now where is it?"

"It is in a place that is well hidden," Nathan began, "There is a cave on the mountain just north of Bryn Mawr. One could walk by it a hundred times and not know it was there. That is where it is hidden."

"It's on Mount Savage?" Dayan asked.

The man nodded.

"You're certain no one has found this place?" Kaylyn demanded.

"Absolutely," Hawk answered, "The entrance is well concealed."

"Fine, then we can get it and be on our way," the Princess stated.

"It won't be that easy," Nathan cautioned, "All those mirror hunters are not going to simply let you walk away with the prize. Especially Count Gregor or Jaques. You'll need a small army to protect you."

"That is why I am here," Donovan commented.

"You don't understand," Hawk explained, "There are nearly thirty in Jaques's company." "I can deal with them," the dragon countered.

Hawk looked at Donovan. "Gregor has Goblins."

Donovan's eyes closed to slits. Wisps of smoke escaped his mouth. "Filthy monsters," he breathed, "How many does he have?"

Nathan shook his head. "I don't know. Talk around town was there were over a hundred of them," he said, "but there could be more."

"Donovan, they must be dealt with," Dayan stated warily.

The dragon nodded.

"Well, that complicates things a bit," the Princess observed.

"That's not all," Rhys interrupted them, "We have unwanted guests." He pointed to the woods. Out from the trees emerged thirteen dwarves. Each was armed with a sword.

"The dwarves from the tavern," Kaylyn whispered to Donovan.

Bevin and Rhys unsheathed their weapons. Ashe drew his bow and strung an arrow. Dayan pulled his wand from his sleeve. Kaylyn had her bow at the ready. Shamar stood by her side. A battle seemed imminent. Each side eyed the other suspiciously.

Then Kaylyn stepped forward. "Who are you and what do you want here?" she demanded.

"I am Argos, leader of the Avisi clan of dwarves. We seek the same thing you do," answered the tallest of the dwarves.

"We are simple travelers passing through Arcadia," the Princess replied.

"Oh, come now," the tall dwarf answered, "Simple travelers don't come well armed and with a dragon at their side. We both know why we are all here. Just as you, we seek the magic mirror."

"You've come to the wrong place. We don't have it," Kaylyn answered.

"Yes, but you have information as to its location," Argos replied.

"How do you know this?" She challenged him.

"Your conversation in the tavern with mister Hawk," the dwarf pointed at Nathan and Kaylyn. "Dwarves have excellent hearing," he continued, "We need that mirror."

"Why?" the Princess demanded.

"My clan and I are prospectors. We mine the mountains for gold, silver, and precious gems but we can no longer work the mines in our homeland. The people there are at war with each other. We are counted as enemies to all," the tall one explained, "We need that mirror to find a new land for us to work."

"So you've come to steal the mirror from us?" Donovan snarled.

"Steal?" Argos answered, "No, we would rather borrow it for a time. We would return it. We mean you no harm."

"You come to our camp with swords drawn and expect us to believe you simply want to borrow it?" the dragon continued.

"We had no idea if we would be treated as friend or foe. Better to be armed and ready just in case," Argos answered.

Kaylyn signaled her company to lower their weapons.

The tall dwarf turned to his comrades and nodded. The dwarves sheathed their swords. "Is that better?" he asked.

"Much better," Kaylyn said. An idea struck her. "If you truly mean us no harm, then why not join us? In my homeland there are many mountains that could be quarried. We would be glad to share with you," she offered.

Argos eyed Kaylyn, "Do you have the authority to make such an offer?"

"I am Princess Kaylyn of the land of Chimera," she replied, "I speak for my brother the King as well as my people."

Nathan looked at Donovan. "She's a Princess?" he asked with an amazed look.

The dragon smiled and nodded.

The dwarves gathered around their leader and talked. Finally he turned back to the Princess. "You are certain we would be welcome?" he asked.

"Absolutely," she answered.

"Then we accept your offer," the dwarf leader said.

"How do we know we can trust them?" Rhys asked.

"Dwarves are not known to be deceitful," Dayan answered.

"We will make certain of that," the dragon said. Donovan leaned toward the dwarves, "First you will swear allegiance to our King Tyler and to Princess Kaylyn. Only then may you join us. If you break your word, then you will have to deal with me." Small wisps of smoke escaped the dragon's mouth.

Argo came forward and said, "I will gladly swear it." He turned to Kaylyn, "My lady, I speak for my clan. We will serve you and your brother faithfully all our days." One by one the others knelt before the Princess.

Kaylyn looked at Nathan. "You said we needed a small army. Well, now we have one." She thought for a moment, then added, "No pun intended."

She turned to her enlarged company, "We will camp here for the night and begin our quest in the morning. We will march on Mount Savage."

As they began to settle in, Shamar picked up a foul odor in the air. He tensed and looked about but saw nothing. He sniffed the air again but the stench was gone. He intently stared at the woods. The wolf furrowed his brow.

Kaylyn noticed her wolf's worried look. "Shamar, what is it?" she asked.

"I'm not sure," he answered, "I caught a whiff of something but now it is gone."

"Probably a mirror hunter was somewhere nearby," the Princess countered.

Shamar looked into the woods one more time but he saw nothing. "You are probably right," he stated. Then He went over and lay down near Kaylyn.

However, the woods were not nearly empty. A set of red eyes had found them. The goblin scout raced off to report to his chieftain. The dragon they had sworn to destroy had been found.

Chapter 14

As dawn began to show its first light, the group awakened and readied themselves for the day's hike. Kaylyn, Dayan, Nathan, Argos, and Donovan sat around a campfire talking.

Dayan cautioned, "We will surely be seen by the mirror hunters. If we go directly up the mountain, they will assume we know something and will follow us. We must appear to be searching for the item just as they are."

"A wise move," Argos stated.

"I agree," Kaylyn added. She looked at Donovan. "And you, my friend, will need to stay here."

"I would think you would want him along," Nathan stated.

The Princess answered, "His presence with us would attract far too much attention."

"But what if we run into trouble?" Hawk argued.

"How far is it to the cave?" Donovan asked.

"It is a little over two leagues north of the town," the man replied.

"That's not too far," Donovan assured him, "If you do encounter a problem, Fatima can alert me and I will come."

"I'm sure if we run into any trouble," Kaylyn smiled at Nathan, "that our small army, as you put it, can hold until Donovan comes."

"We should be on our way," Dayan said.

Kaylyn called for the company to gather around her, "We will move to Mount Savage and there we must appear to be searching for the mirror. No one must suspect that we know its real location."

All nodded.

Finally she turned too Ashe. He nervously bit his lip.

"Will I be going?" he asked.

"You will be right at my side," she replied. She then called out, "Nathan, you and Shamar lead the way."

The youth smiled and joined the Princess as they started out on the day's journey.

Kaylyn's host hiked north of Bryn Mawr to Mount Savage. Nathan and Shamar guided the group up the mountain with Fatima flying overhead. The others scattered out and pretended to be searching for the mirror. Along the way they saw some others who were seeking the mirror. Those they passed paid little attention to Kaylyn's group for they appeared to be looking for the mirror. As they climbed the mountain, the Princess noticed the mirror hunters were fewer and fewer.

"Nathan," she called out, "why are there so few people on the mountain?"

"It is haunted," he replied.

"Haunted?" she repeated.

"Yes," Hawk explained, "People who come here tell stories of hearing voices but no one can be seen."

"Have you heard them?" she asked.

"Yes, but I ignore them. They sound threatening but nothing seems to come of it.

Occasionally, I am hit with a small rock or an acorn but nothing more," he explained.

"That sounds a bit familiar," Kaylyn thought. As they moved up the mountain they began to pass through a large stand of trees. The forest soon surrounded them. It was then that the voices began.

"Go away!" one said.

"You are not welcome in this forest!" came a second.

Kaylyn stopped and looked at her companions. The dwarves seemed to be unnerved by the voices. Bevin and Rhys were moving cautiously with their hands on their swords. Ashe had his bow in hand. Only Dayan seemed unfazed. An acorn then fell at Kaylyn's feet. She stopped and looked up. She saw two raccoons sitting on a large branch of a tree. She smiled.

"You two come down here right now!" she called to them.

The raccoons looked at each other then back at the Princess. They did not move.

"Ashe, do you see those two raccoons sitting on that limb?" she asked.

"Yes, my lady," he answered.

"Can you please place an arrow in the trunk of the tree just to the left of them?" she requested. The youth nodded, "As you wish." He pulled an arrow from his quiver and laced it to the bow. He drew the bow, aimed, and let the arrow fly. It smacked into the trunk right next to the raccoons.

"My archer's next arrow will hit one of the two of you!" the Princess called out, "Now come down here.".

The raccoons looked at each other one more time but did not move.

"Ashe," she ordered the boy, "Ready your bow."

"Alright! Alright! We're coming down," one of the raccoons said.

Nathan and the dwarves were astonished. "Ah! Talking animals in Arcadia. Who would have thought it?" Dayan smiled.

The raccoons scampered down the tree and stood before the Princess with a shamefaced look. One was a bit taller than the other and looked to be older as his fur had a grey tint to it.

"I believe I have found your ghosts," Kaylyn said to Nathan.

"We meant no harm to you. We were only trying to scare you away," the taller raccoon stated, "We are just trying to keep humans off the mountain so they won't hunt my clan."

"How many are you?" the Princess asked.

"Nearly a dozen," came the reply from the graying animal.

"We aren't here to hunt," Kaylyn explained, "We seek another prize."

"The magic mirror," the elder raccoon smiled, "We have heard others that we scared away from the mountain speaking of it."

"Thank you for frightening them off," the Princess smiled, "Hopefully it will make our job easier."

The older raccoon asked, "How did you know we could speak?"

"In my homeland we have many talking animals," Kaylyn answered, "It was just a hunch."

"Where is this place?" the graying one asked.

"Chimera," Kaylyn replied.

"Are those animals hunted as we are?" the younger raccoon spoke up.

"No, they are protected by our people," the Princess stated.

"That must be a wonderful place to live," the elder commented.

"Granddaughter, why not invite them to join us?" Dayan suggested, "I'm sure they would be welcome in Chimera and they could possibly help us now."

"How?" Kaylyn asked.

"Let them continue their ghostly activities. It may keep people away from the mountain," he answered.

"Oh, yes, please let us go with you to Chimera," the elder raccoon pleaded, "We will do all we can to scare everyone away."

"So be it," she said to the raccoons.

They smiled and scampered off. The elder called out, "We'll be sure no one comes near the mountain!"

Kaylyn smiled. She looked at Nathan. "We've been walking for hours now. How much farther is this cave?" she asked.

Jonas grinned. "It is just a few steps away. Follow me," he said and he led them to a small meadow.

Nathan stopped. "Look to your left," he requested.

The Princess turned and studied the area before her. All she could see was an open area that touched a rock outcrop. The rock had some heavy underbrush surrounded by trees. She gave Nathan a puzzled look.

Hawk walked over to the bushes and pulled them out of the way to reveal an opening into the mountain.

"I told you it was well hidden," he announced.

Kaylyn looked at the cave. It truly was well concealed.

"The real question is has anyone else found it?" Dayan asked.

Nathan pointed at the ground. "The dirt is undisturbed." he said.

The Princess turned to the dwarf leader, "Argos, would you ask some of your clan to patrol the area? We don't need anyone stumbling upon us here."

"It will be done, my lady," he answered. He hurried off.

"Bevin, Rhys, you two keep Ashe here and guard the entrance," she continued.

The two soldiers and the young recruit took up position.

"Shall we go see the mirror?" Dayan asked.

"Of course," Hawk answered, "But we will need a torch."

Dayan smiled and drew his wand from his coat sleeve. "I believe this will do," he said.

Nathan was puzzled as he saw the wizard begin to mumble. Suddenly the end of his wand began to glow.

"I believe this will provide us with enough light," the magician said and he motioned them to go forward.

With that Dayan, Nathan, and Kaylyn entered the cave. It took a few moments for their eyes to adjust to the darkened surroundings. The Princess could make out that the cavern was long and narrow.

"How far back is the mirror?" she asked.

"Not far," the man replied, "The cave opens out just ahead. The mirror is hidden just to the right of the opening."

With Dayan's wand providing just enough light they made their way to an open area where the cave seemed to branch out in several directions. Nathan turned the corner to his right and stopped.

He smiled. "Here it is," he announced.

Kaylyn and Dayan looked. They saw a very small, ordinary looking mirror leaning against the wall of the cave. It stood half as tall as one of the dwarves. It had an oval shape framed with wood.

"Not very impressive," Kaylyn observed, "I was expecting something bigger and more elaborate. This barely comes up to my knees."

"Granddaughter, size matters not," Dayan said, "The enchantment is what makes it so important."

The Princess nodded. "How does it work?" she asked.

"A simple rhyme," the wizard answered.

"Not the mirror, mirror on the wall...," Kaylyn whined.

Dayan simply smiled.

"Shall we ask it something?" Hawk suggested.

"We could," the sorcerer responded, "but we would only get an evil answer." Dayan looked at Kaylyn and Nathan. He saw they looked a bit disappointed. "Give me some time," he said, "I believe I have an enchantment that can fix this."

"Agreed," the Princess stated.

"Help me move it near the entrance where I can have some good light," Dayan requested.

Nathan picked up the mirror and the trio moved back to the entrance of the cave.

"How long will this take?" Kaylyn asked.

"I'm not sure," the wizard answered, "It might be a few hours or it could be longer. It depends upon the strength of the curse the witch put on it." The Princess looked at the sky. The sun was low in the west. "It will be dark soon. We should camp here for the night." she suggested, "There's no sense in trying to get down off this mountain in the dark."

She saw her falcon in a nearby tree. "Fatima!" she called out, "Fly to Donovan and tell him we will be camping here for the night."

"As you wish," she replied as she opened her wings and soared into the sky.

Chapter 15

Meanwhile, in the dark woods outside of Bryn Mawr, the goblin scout hurried to report to his leader. As he approached the camp, he noticed several humans and their tents. He growled as he passed them. "Worthless garbage," he muttered. He had barely been able to tolerate the one called Gregor in the camp but now all these other humans from Jaques followers angered him. He did not approve of this arrangement made with them, but now he smiled because he knew the information he had could end this alliance.

He soon spotted his chieftain sitting with the one called Count Gregor. Another gaudily dressed human stood nearby. "That obviously is Jaques," he thought. He gritted his teeth as he approached them.

"Master Kracos," he panted as he ignored the humans, "I have found what we seek." The evil monster looked up, "You have found the mirror?"

"We no longer have need of the mirror," the scout continued with a wry smile.

Kracos stared at his minion with a puzzled look.

"I have found the dragon," the scout reported.

"You're certain?" the goblin chief stood up.

"Yes," the scout answered, "He is the one called Donovan."

Kracos grinned evilly. "He's here and not in his homeland?"

"Yes, master," the scout smiled.

"Where is he?" the goblin leader demanded.

"With a group of humans and dwarves," the scout went on, "They seek the mirror. I heard them say something about searching the mountains to the north."

"Then we shall find them there," Kracos growled, "It is time to destroy our greatest foe." He turned to the rest of the horde, "Make ready to move!"

With that order the goblins began to arm themselves.

Count Gregor stood. "What are you doing?" he demanded.

"We go to slay our enemy," Kracos answered.

"You are supposed to be helping me find that mirror!" the Hun roared.

"You have enough help," the goblin leader pointed at Jaques and his men.

"You will do as I say!" Gregor yelled angrily.

"No one orders me about!" the goblin leader growled. He picked up his axe and threateningly pointed it at the Hun.

The Count did not back down. The goblin was taller and more muscular than the Hun but Gregor was fearless. He drew his sword.

The goblins began muttering and evilly eying the humans in their midst. Some circled the men with their axes drawn at the ready. The men began to unsheathe their blades.

Jaques could see a bloodbath was about to happen so he stepped between Gregor and Kracos. "Great Goblin Warrior, why must you go?" he asked, trying to calm the situation.

Kracos stared at Jaques for a moment and then said, "This dragon killed our protector years ago. We have sworn an oath to destroy him."

"Protector?" Jaques questioned, "Might I ask who that might have been?"

"Yes," the goblin leader answered, "A powerful witch named Lady Cynan. This Dragon turned her to stone."

"So you have vowed vengeance on him," Jaques commented and slickly added, "A noble gesture on your part."

"It is not a noble gesture as you put it," Kracos answered, "It is what we will do or die trying."

"This is not part of our agreement," Gregor angrily snapped.

Kracos stared at Gregor. "It is now," he answered with a snarl. "We will return when the dragon is dead. Then we will help you find your

precious mirror," he mockingly added.

He turned to his hoard and held his axe

above his head. "Death to the dragon!" he howled.

The other goblins roared their approval. They

marched toward the mountains to the north.

Chapter 16

As the first light of dawn crept over the mountain, Dayan found Kaylyn and Nathan sitting by a small campfire. She saw him approaching and stood.

"Well, sir, has the curse been lifted?" she asked.

"I'm sorry child, no." he answered, shaking his head, "I have tried everything I know to do. It is as if the witch locked the curse within the mirror itself."

"So it still gives evil answers," Kaylyn sighed.

"Not exactly," the wizard answered, "I was able to change the curse a bit."

The Princess frowned.

Dayan explained, "Now the answer given by the mirror may have a double meaning. The answer could have a good or an evil meaning. It will depend upon how carefully the question is worded."

Kaylyn blinked, "But you spent the entire night working on it."

Dayan could sense the frustration in his granddaughter's voice. "It is the best I can do at this time.," he spoke softly, "If I can get to my sorcerer's texts, I may be able to do more but those books are not here with me. They are at my hovel."

"Then let's head for your house," she stated.

"Princess, the others hunting this thing are not going to let you leave with it. It may not be too large but it will not easily be concealed and even if we were able to, once they see us start down the mountain they will assume we have found it. Word will spread quickly. We'll be hounded every step of the way. We may even have to fight our way out. Gregor and Jaques alone will kill for it," Nathan warned.

"He's right," Dayan added.

"Then how do we get this mirror home?" Kaylyn asked.

"We need to do something that would make everyone stop looking for it," Hawk stated, "If it was gone, everyone would leave."

Dayan brightened. "Gone or destroyed," he said.

The others looked at him.

"I have an idea," he continued, "I have an old mirror at the house that is just about the same size. I could place an enchantment on it to make it appear to be this mirror. "

"How does that help us?" Kaylyn asked.

"I'll take my mirror to Bryn Mawr and destroy it in front of the people there. If they believe it has been destroyed, the mirror hunters will go home," the wizard explained.

"That just might work," Kaylyn smiled.

"But the people will be angry that you have destroyed the mirror!" Hawk argued.

"Not if they know who I am. They dare not interfere with King Aragon's Wizard," Dayan answered.

"But what if they do not believe you are the wizard?" Nathan argued.

"Donovan will accompany me to the town and appear to be under my control. No one would dare challenge me with a dragon at my side," the wizard replied. He turned to Kaylyn, "What do you think?"

"It's our best chance to get this thing home without a fight," she answered, "We'll stay here and continue to pretend to be looking for the mirror. Hopefully we can keep fooling people and not draw any attention to ourselves."

"Your little raccoon friends should increase their ghostly activities," Nathan added.

"I'll get word to them to do so," Kaylyn stated.

"Granddaughter, I would like to have Nathan to accompany me," Dayan requested, "He can help carry my mirror and I believe he can be of some assistance once in the village."

The Princess looked at Nathan, "Your service would greatly be appreciated."

"Agreed," he said.

"Grandfather, I would like to have my falcon also go with you. She can warn you if she sees anyone moving against you and Donovan." she requested.

The wizard smiled and said, "Thank you."

With that Dayan and Nathan began to make their way down the mountain with Fatima watching from above.

By mid morning they were approaching Dayan's hut. Donovan saw them coming and went to meet them.

"Is everything alright?" he asked. He was obviously concerned. "Fatima brought me word that you were going to camp on the mountain last night," he continued, "Where is Kaylyn and the others?"

"All is well, my friend," the wizard answered. He looked about to be sure they were alone. "The item we have been looking for was just where Nathan said I would be," he stated, "My granddaughter and her friends are looking after things."

"Will they be joining us anytime soon?" the Dragon was anxious, "I have seen a countless number of people searching through this area."

"Not right now," Dayan explained, "We need a way to rid ourselves of all these other treasure hunters. I believe I have a plan."

"It will be a masterpiece of deception," Nathan stated.

As Dayan explained his plan, the dragon listened with great interest. When the wizard had finished, Donovan simply smiled. "That should do it," he commented.

"Best of all, we can leave without fighting a small war," Dayan added, "Now let's get that mirror of mine and turn it into something magical."

Dayan and Nathan went into the hut and emerged with an old, well worn oval shaped looking glass with a wooden frame.

Donovan looked at the object. "Do you really think people will believe that this is the magic mirror?" he asked, "I mean it really doesn't look anything like I imagined. I thought it would be fancy with engravings and gold trim. "

Dayan shook his head, "I know it seems very simple but this one looks almost exactly like the real one."

"But can we really fool everyone with this?" Donovan argued.

"The only people who know exactly what the mirror looks like are Snow White and the three thieves. Snow White is not here. Two of the thieves are in prison, and the third thief has fled the country." Nathan explained, "So no one here knows exactly what it looks like."

"If we tell them this is the mirror," the wizard added, "they will believe it is the mirror, especially when I get done with it. Give me a little time and I will make this a very convincing magic mirror."

Nathan and Donovan stepped back and watched the Wizard go to work.

Chapter 17

As evening approached, Dayan put his plan into action. He had placed an enchantment on his looking glass that made a face appear when he touched the back of it with his wand. It could not answer questions or speak which the Wizard hoped to use to his advantage.

Dayan had Nathan carry the fake mirror. Donovan walked beside Dayan and acted as if he was under a spell and controlled by a magician. Fatima flew above them to warn them of any one who might threaten them.

As they made their way into Bryn Mawr, they attracted a great deal of attention. Seeing a dragon was one thing but what they carried drew the people in. Nathan brandished the mirror about for all to see. Word spread very quickly that the Magic Mirror may have been found. Soon a crowd gathered around the trio.

People began to call out.

"Is that really the mirror?" one yelled.

Another called, "It can't be. It can't be! It's not fancy enough."

"It's too plain to be the mirror," called a third.

"Prove it is the mirror," cried a fourth.

"Yes, yes!" another shouted, "Prove it is the mirror! Ask it a question."

Dayan stopped and held up his hand. The crowd quieted as he began to speak. "I am Dayan, King Aragon's Great Wizard," he announced, "The dragon under my control proves who I am!" He stopped and looked at the crowd around him. He paused and waited for them to quiet. Soon he saw that he had their full attention. "I have found the mirror," he announced proudly.

The crowd cheered.

Again Dayan held up his hand. Once more the crowd quieted. "I bring you grave news," he called out, "This mirror is cursed. It has brought nothing but despair, destruction, and death upon those who question it."

The crowd began to murmur.

"The men who stole this thing took it to many towns where people asked it questions. All the answers turned out to be evil," Dayan continued, "The Duke of Ellington died believing this thing." The people became louder. It was obvious they disagreed with the wizard.

"I will prove it to you," he shouted. The people calmed and watched.

"I will ask it a question and you will see for yourselves that I am speaking the truth," the wizard announced.

Dayan went over and stood by the mirror. He slipped his wand out of his sleeve and brought it near the back of the looking glass. He began to speak,

"Mirror, mirror sitting here,

I ask this question without fear

Can you answer me without evil or deceit

If you cannot, then you cannot speak."

Dayan touched his wand to the back of the glass. A fog appeared on the front. Then a faint face could be seen but no sound could be heard.

The people were astonished.

"Let me show you one more thing," Dayan stated. He spoke to the mirror again,

"Mirror, mirror sitting here

Now I say without fear;

Since evil is the case

Show us your true face."

Again he touched the back with his wand. The fog swirled. It became black and the face changed. A horrible monster appeared. The crowd gasped.

"This evil cannot be allowed to exist any longer!" Dayan cried out. He picked up a large stone and smashed the glass. It fell in pieces on the ground.

The crowd was dumbfounded. No one spoke a word.

"I have destroyed it," Dayan said, "I will report what I have done to King Aragon and send word to Queen Snow White of my actions. Now let us be done with it. Everyone go to your homes wherever they may be and let it be known how evil this thing was."

The people began to disperse. Some were muttering angrily. Others simply shook their heads in disbelief.

Dayan turned to Nathan and Donovan and said, "Let's be gone before they have any time to really think about what has been done. They are shocked by what they have seen. Later they may react in anger. Hopefully most will simply go home."

With that the trio headed out of Bryn Mawr with Fatima flying overhead watching for any trouble.

Chapter 18

Back on Mount Savage, the setting sun began to cast dark shadows across the mountain. The Princess had Rhys patrolling the woods around the camp. Ashe and Shamar were with him.

"What are we looking for?" the boy asked the soldier, "The raccoons surely have scared everyone away."

"As a soldier, one must always expect the unexpected," Rhys replied, "We are looking just in case someone does like Mr. Hawk and ignores the voices. We need to keep our eyes open and our mouths shut. We don't want to give away our position. As a scout we must see but not be seen."

"Oh, okay," Ashe replied and he quieted.

They walked on in silence for some time. Suddenly the wolf stopped. He cocked his head to one side. His nose raised and sniffed the air. He warily looked to his right.

"Shamar, what is it?" Rhys asked in a whisper.

"It's that odor again. The one I detected last night," he quietly replied, "It smells like rotten eggs."

"I smell it, too," Ashe added in a low voice.

Ashe saw Rhys take a deep breath. Then the young soldier looked about nervously. His eyes widened.

"What is it?" the boy asked.

"Goblins," came the answer as Rhys pointed down the mountainside.

Climbing over the rocks and moving toward them was a host of green monsters. The beasts were chanting, "Kill the dragon. Kill the dragon." Ashe saw the goblin horde. He shook at the sight of them. "What will we do?" he asked.

Rhys gulped. He turned to the youth, "We need to get to the Princess! We need to warn her."

"What about Donovan?" the boy nervously asked.

Rhys then looked at the young wolf, "Shamar, can you get down the mountain and warn Donovan that a Goblin army is here?"

The wolf nodded and set off.

Shamar quickly moved from one hiding place to another, trying to stay out of sight of the Goblins. The dense undergrowth and bushes helped hide him from the beasts. He moved through their midst. He soon reached a point where he saw that he was just behind the monsters. He took a deep breath and raced off down the mountainside. His final movement caught the eyes of one of the Goblins.

"Master Kracos," the beast called out, "There is an animal that is running away from us. Shall I go after it and kill it?"

The Goblin chief stopped and held up his hand. The green horde halted their march. Kracos looked and saw the young wolf making his way in the distance. He watched for a moment and then said, "No, we have simply scared an animal out of these woods. Let it go. We have a sworn oath to fulfill." He held his axe above his head and shook it. "Onward!" he cried, "Kill the dragon,"

The goblins began to move and took up their chant, "Kill the dragon! Kill the Dragon!"

Rhys and Ashe watched to be sure Shamar made it through the enemy lines. They then hurried back up the mountain side. They exited the trees at a run. Kaylyn was at the mouth of the cave and saw them hurrying toward her. She frowned. "This can't be good," she thought as they approached.

"Princess!" Rhys reported nearly out of breath, "Goblins! Goblins coming up the mountain! They are chanting death to the dragon."

Upon hearing the news, she muttered, "I should have known." She took a deep breath. "How many are there?" she asked.

"I couldn't get an accurate count for the trees had them scattered about," Rhys reported, "but I would estimate well over one hundred."

Kaylyn turned to Argos, "Call in your clan. Bring them up here by the mouth of the cave. We may need to hold this ground until Donovan arrives."

Rhys stepped up to the Princess. "I will defend you to your right," he solemnly stated.

Bevin took up a position on her left. "And I will be here," he gravely added.

Kaylyn's eyes then found Ashe. She looked at her young recruit. "I didn't plan for you to risk your life but now I'm afraid that has been forced on us. Stay by my side no matter what happens." She instructed Ashe, "You must show no fear. Goblins can sense it and it makes them bolder. Being unafraid unnerves them. Be ready to use your bow."

The youth nodded. "I only have a few arrows," he nervously said, "What do I do when I run out?"

"Pull from my quiver," she replied.

"But you will run out, too," he protested.

"No, I won't" she shook her head, "I have a magical quiver that never runs out of arrows. It once belonged to my Grandmother. My Grandfather, Dayan, gave it to her."

The boy smiled weakly. "Do you think we have a chance?" he asked.

"If we can only hold until Donovan comes," she answered.

"Your majesty, the enemy approaches," Bevin reported as the goblins began making their way out of the trees onto the meadow.

Chapter 19

Kaylyn took a deep breath as she saw the goblin army assemble before her defenders. She could see that they were greatly outnumbered. A look of determination crossed her face.

"Stand at the ready!" she ordered. The dwarves drew their swords. Bevin and Rhys unsheathed their blades. Ashe stood by her side with an arrow strung in his bow.

Then the green monsters began to stand aside allowing one to step forward. Kaylyn realized this one must be their leader.

Kracos strode to the front of his army. He stopped and lowered his weapon. He looked at the humans and dwarves defending the cave. He shook his head and called out, "We have no quarrel with you humans or dwarves! We come for the dragon!"

Kaylyn smiled because she realized that may have bought them some time. "There is no dragon here," she answered.

"Where is he?" Kracos demanded, "We know he was with you! Our scout has seen him!"

"There is no dragon with us!" the Princess answered.

Kracos angered. "We know he is your friend so we will keep you here and wait for him to return." He turned to his green horde, "We will await the dragon!"

The monsters took up their chant, "Kill the dragon! Kill the dragon!"

Kaylyn looked at her defenders. "They will not attack us right now," she said.

Argos frowned. "Your majesty, they could easily overwhelm us," he said, "Why wouldn't they attack?"

She spoke to the dwarves, "We have seen this behavior before. They are after Donovan." She could see they were not convinced so she added, "We fought goblins in our homeland. They were after our friend, Donovan. When they attacked him, they took little notice of our army. They will leave us alone as long as we do not provoke them."

The dwarves put away their weapons.

There was a stirring in the goblin host. The goblin scout made his way to his chieftain. He pointed toward the cave. "Master Kracos, look behind the humans. There is a mirror at the cave's entrance," he said.

Kracos squinted in the failing light of day but soon spied the object. "Well, well," he said, "That is why they were ready to do battle. They have found the Magic Mirror. We shall fulfill two duties on this day."

The Goblin leader then called out, "I see you have found the Magic Mirror! Why not give it to us now and save yourselves the trouble of dying for it." Kaylyn was surprised but defiantly answered, "We found it. It is rightfully ours. It stays with us." Kracos frowned, "Then I suppose you will have to deal with Gregor and his friends. I'm sure Gregor, Jaques, and his band of killers will take the matter up with you. I will send for them to join us."

He turned to his scout. "Go back to camp," he ordered, "Tell Gregor and Jaques we have located the mirror."

The scout asked, "But, Master shouldn't we just take the mirror from the humans and dwarves? We could easily have it in a matter of minutes."

"No, I will not squander one of our clan for that thing," the goblin leader stated, "Let Gregor and Jaques attempt to take it. Let them waste human blood getting it. We will fight the dragon when he returns. Now go. Tell Gregor and Jaques that if they hurry, they might be here by sunrise."

The scout set off.

The young wolf had made his way down the mountain as quickly as he could. As he approached Dayan's house, he saw Donovan, Nathan, and Dayan returning from Bryn Mawr. He raced to them to report.

Donovan saw Shamar and sensed something was wrong. He hurried ahead to meet the young wolf.

"Shamar, what is it?" he called out as he approached the animal.

The young wolf caught his breath and replied, "Goblins! A goblin army is on the mountain and they seek you. They were heading in the direction of the Princess."

Dayan approached and heard the news. "It appears the battle is being forced upon us. Those monsters need to be dealt with."

"I agree," the dragon answered with a snarl. "Shamar, how many were there?" he asked the wolf.

"Well over one hundred," came the reply.

"That's also the number being bantered about in town," Nathan added as he joined them.

"I can go and destroy them," the dragon snarled as he opened his wings.

"Or you could fly right into a trap," Dayan cautioned, "and what if they are holding Kaylyn and the others as hostages? They could force you to surrender to them. Your death will do Chimera no good."

"I can't just do nothing," Donovan argued.

"Send Fatima ahead to scout the situation," Dayan suggested, "It won't take her long to fly up there and back. She might even be able to get a message to Kaylyn. When we know more, we can plan how to deal with those evil beasts."

Donovan reluctantly agreed and called Fatima. She had landed in a nearby tree.

"Fatima, fly over the cave area and find out what you can. If you can speak to Kaylyn without endangering yourself, let her know we will come as soon as we can," Dayan requested.

Donovan added, "Please hurry."

The falcon nodded and flew off. It took her only a few minutes to reach the cave. She circled and saw that the goblins had Kaylyn and the others trapped near the mouth of the cave. She circled the area trying to get a count of the number of goblins but they were moving about making it difficult to get an accurate number. She decided to take a chance and she landed in one of the trees near the mouth of the cavern. The Princess saw the falcon. She eased her way over near the tree trying not to draw any attention to herself or her friend.

"Princess," the falcon whispered, "Are you alright?"

"For the moment," she answered quietly, "They want Donovan and not us but they know he is our friend so they are waiting for him to return. Of more concern right now is that the goblins have sent for Gregor, Jaques, and his mob. I'm sure they mean to take the mirror by force."

"I will report it to Donovan and your grandfather," the falcon stated.

"If you can, let me know what they plan to do." The Princess requested.

"I will do my best," Fatima answered. She opened her wings and flew into the sky. Kaylyn watched for any reaction by the goblins but there was none. She breathed a sigh of relief.

The falcon glided her way into the valley and to Dayan's home. She found her waiting friends and made her report.

"As best I can tell there are well over one hundred of the goblins," Fatima stated, "but worse is the goblins have called for Gregor and someone called Jaques to join them," The bird answered.

Nathan gulped. "That would be Jaques and his marauders," he gasped, "They are known as merciless killers. They want that mirror badly."

"We need to stop them," Donovan growled.

The wizard turned to Nathan. "Is there a way up the east side of the mountain?" he asked.

"Yes," Hawk answered, "there is a trail but it will take us some time to find it and make the climb. It could be dawn when we reach the cave area." Dayan scratched his chin. "That could work to our advantage. The sun would be in their eyes." He turned to Donovan. "We must take them by surprise;" he offered, "The goblins will probably be expecting you to fly in and hopefully Gregor and his band are not expecting you at all."

"What are you thinking?" Donovan asked his old friend.

"We do what they do not expect," Dayan answered, "We attack at dawn."

"But there are only three of us!" Nathan protested.

"You forget that he is a dragon and I am a wizard," Dayan responded, "We will more than outnumber them."

A puzzled look crossed Hawk's face.

The wizard simply smiled. "Fatima, do you think you can get back to the princess and tell her what we plan to do?"

"I will try," she replied.

Then an idea struck Dayan. "Fatima, I have one more task for you," he said, "On your way, see if you can find the raccoons. Tell them that humans are coming up the mountain. They must do their best ghostly impressions and tell them to pretend they are the spirits of people killed by Jaques' band."

The bird grinned, "That should put a real scare into them." She opened her wings and soared into the air.

"It will be dark soon. We need to be on our way," Donovan stated.

The trio set off.

Chapter 20

The Goblin Scout made his way down the mountain. He made no attempt to hurry as he did not like the humans and he felt the goblins should have seized the mirror but his leader had given him orders so he was bound to carry them out.

As he approached the camp, he saw Gregor and Jaques sitting by the fire.

"Lazy humans," he muttered as he approached them. He stopped by the fire and said, "Master Kracos sends you word that the Magic Mirror has been located."

Gregor and Jaques stood.

"Where is it?" Gregor demanded.

"It is near a cave on the mountain," he answered. He waited a moment and then he added, "It is guarded by a band of humans and some dwarves."

"Not for long," Jaques stated. "Comrades, to arms!" he called out, "We go to claim the mirror!" The thugs and killers gathered their weapons.

Gregor turned to the scout. "Lead the way," he ordered.

The Goblin snarled but set off with the humans following him.

As Fatima made her flight back to Kaylyn, she spied the graying raccoon sitting on a tree limb. She landed near him and told him what needed to be done.

The elder raccoon responded, "You can be sure we will do our best."

The falcon then finished her flight and circled above the now sleeping goblins. She landed in the tree near the cave. Kaylyn quietly approached.

"Dayan and Donovan will attack at dawn," the bird whispered.

"Attack?" the Princess questioned, "With what?"

"Dayan said that we will outnumber our foe," the bird answered.

The Princess shook her head. "I don't see how…" she breathed.

"Remember he is a wizard," Fatima stated.

"Yes, I'm sure that helps but I still don't see how," she replied.

"Just be ready to fight at dawn," the bird quietly said.

Donovan, Dayan, and Nathan found the trail up the eastern slope of Mount Savage. Nathan guided them but the pathway was a far easier climb than they had expected. A full moon gave them a great deal of light and aided them. They worked their way along until they reached a point overlooking the cave area.

"We will wait here until sunrise," Dayan whispered as he looked at the sky. There was a hint of light in the east. "It shouldn't be long."

The Goblin Scout led Gregor and his band up the mountain. He made no attempt to hurry in spite of Gregor's constant growling that they needed to move faster. All was well until they reached a stand of trees halfway up the trail. Then the voices began.

At first the evil company heard what sounded like whispers coming from all around them.

"What is that?" Jaques asked aloud.

Gregor stopped and looked about. "It is nothing but the wind," he answered.

Then the voices got louder.

"Go back!" came one.

"Death awaits you!" came another,

The men slowed and pulled their swords. They nervously looked from side to side but saw no one.

"That's not the wind!" Jaques said.

"Doom! Doom!" came a third voice.

"Your destruction is but a few steps away!" a fourth called out.

Suddenly it seemed as if the entire forest erupted into voices.

"The grave awaits you!" came another voice.

The raccoons began to chant, "Death! Death! Death!"

"Who is there?" cried one of the men nervously.

"This is the forest of lost souls. We are the spirits of those you have murdered," came the answer, "Your judgement day is here!".

"Your souls are now required of you!" came a dark, deep voice.

"I want no part of this!" yelled one frightened man as he threw down his sword and fled down the mountain. Quickly several others followed. The voices took up a chant, "Death! Doom! Destruction!"

Two more men fled in terror.

"Get your men under control," Gregor ordered Jaques, "Get them out of these trees." Jaques gathered up what was left of his gang and raced to exit the forest. The voices did not follow them. The men stopped and caught their breath. Jaques quickly counted the men he still had with him. He found he had only twenty one. He turned to Gregor and said, "I still have more than enough to take the mirror."

"How much farther?" Gregor demanded of the Goblin.

"It is just over this next rise," he answered.

"Good!" Gregor smiled, "The sun will be up soon and we can deal with whoever has the mirror." They moved over the rise and into the Goblin camp. In the trees the Raccoons gathered around their elder.

"We did the best we could," he said, "I just hope it is enough to help the Princess."

Kaylyn had watched as a band of humans joined the goblins. She assumed it was Gregor and Jaques. "Not as many as we were told," she thought. She looked to the eastern sky. It was brightening. She awakened her troops and readied them for battle.

As the sun began to peek over the mountains, the goblins began to stir. Jaques looked up at the band of defenders. He smiled for he thought little of those who were standing against him. Entire cities had fallen to him and his men. What could a few humans and dwarves do? He said to Gregor, "Let me speak to them. I think I can get them to surrender without a fight."

Gregor laughed, "They hold the high ground but go ahead. Waste your voice. It will just give me more time to plan an attack."

Jaques stepped out in front of the camp.

"I am Jaques the Vile," he loudly announced, "You stand no chance against me! I have destroyed cities! Kings have fallen before me! I have killed without mercy!" He looked to see if the defenders were listening. "People tremble at the mention of my name. I am feared wherever I go," he arrogantly bragged. He held out his hands and continued, "But today I feel merciful. Turn the Magic Mirror over to me and I will let you live! Of course, you will be sold as slaves but you will live!" He smiled broadly. "Today I am merciful! Give me the mirror and live!"

"I've heard just about enough," Kaylyn growled as she strung an arrow to her bow. Jaques did not see the girl and he went on, "Bring me the mirror now and live! I swear to you that not a hair on your heads will be harmed. I await your surrender." He turned and smiled at Gregor. "I believe they are listening," he proclaimed.

The Princess swiftly aimed and loosed the arrow. It found its target. It struck Jaques in the chest and he fell to the ground dead.

"You have our answer!" Kaylyn yelled.

Gregor stepped forward. "Attack them," he ordered Jaques' men. The marauders were shocked and angered to see their leader cut down. They sprang up the slope only to be met by the dwarves. Bevin and Rhys guarded the Princess while she and Ashe loosed arrows at their attackers. The number of marauders quickly dwindled.

Gregor roared at Kracos, "What are you waiting for? Send in your goblins! Kill them all!" Kracos growled, "Stupid humans! They can't even take a woman, some boys, and a few dwarves." He reluctantly turned to his clan. "Forward!" he ordered.

At that moment Donovan took to the air with the sun at his back. He was unseen in the bright morning light. He let loose blasts of fire which caught some of the goblins. The beasts hesitated for they could not see their opponent. To draw their attention away from Kaylyn and the dwarves, the dragon landed behind them, with flames blasting and claws slashing.

Kracos yelled, "Kill the dragon!" and the goblins forgot about Kaylyn's troop and turned their attention to Donovan. They went at him from all sides.

"We've got to help Donovan!" Kaylyn ordered the dwarves. "Argos, attack the goblins!" The dwarves drove into the beasts lashing at them with their blades. Kaylyn and Ashe loosed arrow after arrow taking many of the monsters down but their numbers were great.

Dayan then came to Kaylyn's side. He began to wave his wand and chant. Suddenly there seemed to be hundreds of dwarves.

Kaylyn's mouth fell open. "How did you do that?" she asked.

"They aren't real! They are a mirage! The goblins will not know which ones are real and which ones are not," he answered as he again took up a chant. Soon rocks were flying from the ground and smashing into the monsters. The goblins became utterly confused. Rocks were hitting them. Ghostly dwarves that did not die when sliced by an axe seemed to be everywhere, and worst of all there was a dragon bent on destroying them all. A few began to back away and make their escape. In the melee three of Jaques men made their way near the cave. Two jumped up and swung their swords at Kaylyn. Bevin and Rhys went to her defense. Blades smashed at each other. The two youths fiercely defended their Princess. Dayan saw what was happening and quickly turned the attackers' swords into loaves of bread. Bevin and Rhys then wasted little time dealing with them.

The third man appeared and came for the Princess while her two protectors were busy. He knocked her to the ground. Ashe tried to step between Kaylyn and her attacker. The murderer used the back of his hand to knock the boy to the ground.

"Ashe!" Kaylyn cried, "Get away!"

She tried to get up but her attacker brought his sword to bear on her. Just as he was about to strike, a grey ball of fur smashed into him, knocking him back. Shamar stood between the Princess and her assailant. He growled.

The killer grinned and turned his sword toward the wolf. Then, seemingly out of nowhere, Nathan raced in and tackled the thug. He drove him hard into the ground and the attacker hit his head on a rock. Nathan rose up to strike the man.

"It won't do any good," Shamar stopped him, "He's unconscious."

Nathan looked and saw the man was out cold.

Gregor looked about and saw his allies were about to be killed or on the run. He realized the battle would soon be lost and he had no chance to get the mirror. He started to push his way through the throng and to escape.

Dayan saw him fleeing. "Stop him!" he cried, "If he gets away, he will return with a Hun army!"

Ashe reached out and grabbed an arrow from Kaylyn's quiver. As he stood up, he strung it and quickly took aim. He loosed the arrow. For what seemed like minutes, it flew straight and true. Then the arrow found its target. Gregor hit the ground with a thud. He would bother them no more.

Kracos has worked his way close to Donovan and came face to face with him. He roared, "You will die, dragon! This is for all my clan and my mistress!" He raised his axe above his head. Donovan let loose a sheet of flames. When the smoke cleared, all that was left was a pile of ash.

With that, the rest of the goblins began to flee.

Kaylyn looked to see Donovan standing in the middle of the meadow surrounded by dead

goblins. Her eyes then found Argos and the
dwarves. She quickly counted and was relieved to
come up with the number thirteen. To her right she
saw Bevin and Rhys. In front of her stood Shamar
and Nathan. Then she found Ashe. She breathed a
sigh of relief.

The youth smiled at her. "Did we win?" he
asked.

She reached out and hugged him. "Yes, we
did," she answered.

"Your highness," Donovan said as he
approached, "That was an amazing shot. You hit
Gregor while he was on the run and nearly
surrounded by goblins."

"That wasn't me,' she answered, "It was
Ashe." She pointed to the youth.

The dragon looked at the boy and grinned.
"Now I'm glad he bested you in that archery
contest," he said to the Princess.

"I am too," she smiled.

"Did I do well?" Ashe asked.

"As good as the best Chimeran soldier," Donovan pronounced as he patted the youth on the . head.

The boy beamed.

Chapter 21

Two days later, the weary band trudged back into Rockwood. Fatima had been sent ahead to announce their coming and there was a crowd lining the streets up to the castle. They were cheered as they made their way through the city. Tyler was relieved to see his sister but also surprised by the number of others she brought home. He met them in the castle courtyard. Kaylyn saw her brother and halted her troop.

"Your highness, I have returned with our prize. This is the magic mirror," she announced as she pointed to a plain looking mirror held by two of the dwarves.

"You are certain?" the King asked.

"Yes, my brother, this is it," she answered.

"We heard it had been destroyed by someone in Bryn Mawr," Tyler responded.

"That would be me, your highness," the old wizard stated.

Tyler stared at the man. "Sir, you look familiar to me. Do I know you from somewhere? Have we met?" he asked.

Donovan stepped to the wizard's side. "Your majesty, this is your grandfather," he said.

"Dayan!" Tyler shouted. He grinned as he reached out and took the wizard's hand. "It has been a long time."

"Too long," Dayan answered, "but you do remember me."

"Yes, we must talk. There has been much that has happened here," the king stated.

"There has been much that we have encountered, too," the magician countered as he pointed to all those near him. "This is a most amazing group. You need to meet them."

"Of course," Tyler said and he turned back to his sister, "Please introduce me to your new companions."

Kaylyn smiled and began, "First I would like to tell you that Rhys, Bevin, Fatima, and Shamar risked their lives for me. They have served me well."

Tyler looked at the four. He nodded his head. "You have each carried out my commands from when you left. I shall see to it that you are well rewarded."

The four bowed and said in unison, "Thank you, your Majesty."

"And our great friend, Donovan," Kaylyn added, "He kept us safe and helped destroy a goblin army."

"How can I repay you?" the King asked.

"Your friendship is reward enough," the dragon stated.

Kaylyn turned to the others in her company and said, "Let me introduce you to Nathan Hawk." Nathan bowed before the King.

"This is Nathan Hawk? I thought you sought a bird," Tyler said.

"So did we until we met this amazing gentleman," the Princess stated, "He has been of great service to us. He has but one request and that is to ask a question of the mirror."

"Might I ask what knowledge you seek from the mirror?" the King asked Nathan.

The man lowered his head and explained, "As a child I was sold into slavery to pay a debt owed by my father. I was fortunate enough to have been purchased by a kind and generous man. Years later, upon his death, I was set free. I went to my home but my family was gone. I would ask the mirror to help me find them."

Tyler nodded, "It will be done."

"Thank you, sir," came a quiet reply.

Kaylyn then turned to the dwarves. "This is Argos and his Avisi clan. He and his brethren have fought bravely beside me against a horde of goblins and evil men. They seek a land where they can mine for precious metals and stones."

The dwarves knelt before the king. "Please rise," Tyler stated, "It is I who should bow to you. As a reward for your service to my sister, you shall have a place to do your prospecting in our western mountains."

The dwarves smiled and nodded.

Argos spoke up, "We shall share whatever we find with you and your kingdom."

"It is agreed," Tyler said.

The Princess went on, "The raccoons that are with me also helped keep us safe. They are possibly the last talking animals in Arcadia. They seek a home here."

"They shall have it!" Tyler proclaimed, "A place in the north woods."

The raccoons now knelt before their new king.

Finally Kaylyn turned to the young man standing at her side. "And, brother, this courageous young man is Ashe. His bravery and skill with the bow helped us destroy a Bogeyman, defeat the goblins, and end the evil terror of the Hun, Gregor."

"What is his wish?" Tyler asked.

Kaylyn continued, "He is an orphan and needs a home."

"You shall have it," the King said to the youth, "We will search out the best family in Rockwood to adopt you."

"Brother," the Princess interrupted, "I have a request."

"Anything for my sister," he answered.

Kaylyn hesitated for a moment but then spoke out, "I would like to be named as guardian to Ashe."

Tyler smiled at his younger sister, "So you wish to be more than my Captain of the Guard."

The Princess blushed and said, "In this case and for this very special boy, yes."

The King turned to the youth. "I believe you should have a say in this, too," he said, "Would you like Kaylyn to be named as your adopted mother?"

The boy grinned broadly. "Yes!" he cried.

Kaylyn put her arm around the boy and he hugged her.

Epilogue

The next day Tyler, Kaylyn, and Dayan stood before the mirror as it sat in the throne room. Dayan cautioned, "The mirror still has the curse on it. I have only been able to modify it a bit. When the mirror is asked a question, it may answer in a manner that could be interpreted either as good or evil. If the question is very specific, the better the chances are of getting a good answer, however there could still be used for great evil if it falls into the wrong hands."

"Well, all the world thinks this thing was destroyed in Bryn Mawr," Kaylyn observed.

"Yes, but it best be placed where few have any access to it," Tyler stated, "It will be placed in the lowest dungeon of the castle."

"Can we allow Nathan to ask his question before we move it?" Kaylyn requested.

"Bring him in," the King answered.

The Princess went into the hall and returned with Nathan...

"You may ask your question now," Dayan instructed, "but be careful with your wording and be specific. Remember the information this thing gives may be good or evil."

Nathan stood before the mirror for a moment deep in thought. Then he said,"Mirror, mirror on the wall, please listen to my call, grant me one wish that I might see, tell me where my family might be." The mirror fogged and a ghostly face appeared. It said, "In the land of Greece in a town called Smyrna, there you will find your sister Ramona."

Dayan smiled, "I think you got a truthful answer."

Nathan smiled, "Then I shall be on my way."

"I hope you come back," Kaylyn said, "I mean I might set out to find something else someday. Who knows? I might need some help."

Nathan smiled,"You can count on it," he said and he left.

"Now I have one request before I return to Arcadia," Dayan said.

"I was hoping you would stay a while," Tyler sadly said.

"I need to get back to King Aragon. I am his court magician. I am in his debt for all he has done for me," Dayan answered, "But I'm sure he will let me come and visit."

The King smiled. "What is your request?"

"Take me to your grandmother's grave," he said with emotion in his voice, "I must pay my respects."

"Follow me," Tyler said. He and Kaylyn led the wizard outside the city to a small cemetery. There he pointed out a simple marker. Dayan stood by the grave with his head bowed low. Tyler and Kaylyn kept their distance out of respect. He seemed to be talking which puzzled the youths. Finally he stepped back by their side.

"Grandfather," Kaylyn asked, "Were you talking to Grandmother?"

The wizard smiled. "In a way," he answered, "I told her that I would be joining her soon."

"Oh, no, Grandfather," she cried, "We are just getting to know you."

"It may be a while, Granddaughter," he answered, "and we will have time together but the age of magic is coming to a close. The age of science is coming. No one will need magic any longer. It may last longer in Chimera because of all the enchanted creatures that live here but eventually it will end. I will be around for some time yet but someday soon I will no longer be needed. My time will come then."

"Let us make the best use of our time we have together," Tyler said.

And they all lived happily ever after!

Until we meet again…

Made in the USA
Middletown, DE
06 July 2023